Father Roberto and the Missing Money

Two heartwarming cosy mysteries

Stefania Hartley

To all the Fathers Roberto I've ever met.

CONTENTS

1. THE HOLIDAY HEIST

The parish's nativity scene had turned into a monster, Father Roberto thought.

Last Christmas, when he had just joined the parish as a newly ordained priest, the nativity scene had sat comfortably on the altar of one of the side chapels. Now, sitting on wooden boards on metal trestles, it covered the entire chapel. This Bethlehem had sprawled from a village into a metropolis faster than any other settlement on the planet.

Still, the parish's nativity scene looked like a work of art and dedication, Roberto admitted, with no detail overlooked.

The landscape's rocks were made with cork tree bark, moss stood in for the vegetation, and sand made the desert where the three kings travelled on their clay dromedaries. Tiny electric-powered torches lit up cobblers' workshops, smithies, bakeries—each donated by the respective trade associations hundreds of years ago. This year, even a real-life stream gurgled cheerfully, powered by a hidden pump, and small speakers broadcast gentle Christmas music from inside the stable.

All this had required hours of work by dedicated parishioners, and hours of Roberto's time, too, to solve any disagreements between them. As he had arbitrated quarrels over the position of this or that trade's workshop relative to Baby Jesus's manger, he had wondered whether adults were any easier to deal with than children.

But now, at last, the nativity scene was complete, the parishioners who had put it together were still on amicable terms, and all that was missing was the eighteenth-century wax baby Jesus, hand-crafted by one of the specialised master craftsmen whose workshops used to line a nearby street named after them.

Roberto looked with worry at the manger, situated at the top of the miniature town. How was he going to lay Baby Jesus on his crib on Christmas Eve without trampling shepherds and sheep, cobblers and ironmongers?

A litter-picker might just reach, but wouldn't it be disrespectful towards Baby Jesus, especially one of such a venerable age as theirs?

A system of pulleys suspended from the

ceiling could deliver the baby to his crib in comfort and style from the sky. If used during the service, it would have the added bonus of illustrating the baby's heavenly nature in a very visual way. But installing it would be a lot of work, and would possibly be in breach of the building's historical listing.

Another idea came to Roberto: if he could find a way to reach the back of the installation from underneath, he could make a little hatch—just wide enough for his hand and the wax baby to fit through.

Visitors strolled over to admire the installation and dropped coins into the donation box. It was tradition that, at this time of year, people visited Palermo's many churches to admire their nativity scenes.

Roberto didn't think it would be a good idea to crawl under the boards and saw holes in the plywood while visitors were admiring the installation. Instead, he decided to wait until the evening, when the church was closed.

***

Usually, when Roberto came down from the priests' flat to the church after closing time, it was to pray. He loved praying in the peace and silence of the empty church, under the soft light of the tabernacle's candle, without any chance of being disturbed.

But tonight he was on different business. Armed with a saw, hinges, screws and a screwdriver, he would create a hatch so that he could deliver the wax Baby Jesus to his crib without stomping on the entire Bethlehem like Gulliver on Lilliput.

The nativity scene was built on a tiered plywood structure, hidden at the front and sides by a green velvet valance. Roberto's plan was to squeeze under the structure and reach the top tier, where the manger rested, from underneath.

He lifted the valance to inspect the space. An envelope, previously hidden by the valance, lay on the floor, just behind the donation box.

Someone must have tried to post their donation into the box's slot and missed. Roberto picked it up to drop it into the box but stopped. The envelope felt thick and heavy, as if it contained a lot of notes. The donation box had been forced by thieves more than once. Roberto decided it would be safer if he took the envelope upstairs with him as soon as he had finished making the hatch.

***

"I've solved Baby Jesus's problem," Roberto announced to Father Pietro as soon as he stepped back into their flat.

"I thought it was Baby Jesus who had come

into the world to solve our problems, not the other way round," Father Pietro said with a smile.

He turned off the quiz show he was watching on TV and gave Roberto his full attention. Father Pietro's ability to make others feel properly listened to was one of his many gifts. "So, what was Baby Jesus's problem?"

"How He would get to His crib on Christmas Eve without me trampling the whole of Bethlehem. But I've managed to crawl under the scaffolding and instal a hatch by the manger. Then, on Christmas Eve I'll crawl back there, open the hatch, and deliver the baby!"

"I thought it was Mother Mary who delivered the baby," Father Pietro said with a good-humoured smile. "But well done. I knew you'd be an asset to this parish, but I never thought it would be for your handyman skills too."

Roberto smiled. He had always been a bookworm and considered himself lacking in the practical sphere. Today had been his first time to use a saw or a screwdriver and he felt very pleased with himself.

"By the way, I've also found what looks like a very generous donation," Roberto said, handing Father Pietro the envelope. "It had fallen out of the donation box and I thought it would be safer to keep it here overnight."

Father Pietro opened the envelope. Its contents left both priests speechless.

The thickness of the envelope had suggested that there might be many notes, but nothing had prepared them for the fact that each one was a fifty-euro note.

"Who could have given a donation like that?"

Father Pietro nodded gravely. "Someone who has big regrets. Unfortunately, there's a lot of criminality in our neighbourhood, and some people have big weights on their conscience. Sometimes they give money to the church as a way of saying sorry to God."

"But this is a lot of money," Roberto said, still reeling over the amount.

"And yet it might just be a small amount for them."

"Now we can start the church roof's repair works," Roberto said enthusiastically.

"The donor hasn't indicated that the donation should go towards the church roof's repair fund so we'll have to convene a parish council meeting to allocate the funds. There are several projects in the parish in need of money."

Roberto grunted. It was true that the

parish's soup kitchen, the food bank, the children's holiday camp and the pilgrimage fund were always strapped for cash, but the church roof was leaking. "I still think that the roof is a priority."

"Hopefully, the parish council will agree with you. We must always remember that the parish doesn't belong to the priests. It belongs to the parishioners. We are here today but may be transferred to another parish tomorrow," Father Pietro said.

Roberto didn't feel that way. The parish was his home and he felt very protective of it. "How many parishioners have relocated out of our parish during the fifteen years you've been here?" he challenged.

Father Pietro frowned. "The Lord was right when he said that money was a tainted thing. Look at us: we've only just got this money and we are already arguing over it."

Roberto didn't think it was the money's fault; it was more to do with Father Pietro's being a stickler for protocol. But he kept silent.

"First of all," the senior priest continued, "we must take the money to the bank. It's not safe to keep it here, especially after all the robberies we've had recently."

Antique paintings and silverware had been stolen in the last couple of years, forcing the parish to instal security cameras inside the church.

"Yes," Roberto agreed.

"As you've finished the marriage preparation course, could you do it?"

Roberto wished he had twenty more marriage preparation courses, or forty baptisms to celebrate or one hundred confessions to hear—any reason to turn down Father Pietro's request. Even a funeral would be preferable to the stress of carrying all that cash around the streets. "Wouldn't it be safer if we went together? It's a lot of money, and I could get robbed…"

Father Pietro smiled. "How many times have you been robbed since you've come to this parish? Or even in your entire life?"

"None."

"So why should you be now that you are a priest? Priests are not known for carrying large amounts of cash in their wallets."

Roberto nodded but he still wished he didn't have to do this.

***

That night, Roberto didn't sleep well. In one dream, he was travelling on a horse, carrying the king's gold, when he was attacked by some highwaymen. In another dream, he was on board a ship that was attacked by pirates.

By the time he went down to church to celebrate morning Mass, he had already fervently and abundantly prayed for the safe delivery of the money to the bank.

Roberto was getting into his vestments when Father Pietro burst into the sacristy.

"We had another burglary last night," he announced with concern.

"Oh no. What have they stolen this time?"

"This is what I don't understand: they've stolen the painting of our Lady and that of St John the Baptist. They weren't worth much. Why did they bother? Repairing the damage to the window will cost us more than the value of the paintings," Father Pietro said, scratching his chin.

Roberto immediately thought back to the envelope with the cash. If thieves were so desperate that they had put so much effort into stealing two cheap paintings, how much more energy would they put into stealing all that cash from him?

During Mass, Roberto pleaded his case with God again, then went upstairs and got ready for his mission. He would not carry the cash in his bag.

He stuffed the envelope into a sock and strapped it to his chest, under his vest. It gave him an unsightly paunch but robbers would have to strip him naked before they'd find his precious cargo. In extreme circumstances, the wad of notes was so thick that it might even double up as a bulletproof vest.

As an additional precaution, he asked to borrow Father Pietro's car so that he didn't have to walk, and planned his escape routes to all the nearest police and carabinieri stations along the way. He imagined being chased by thieves on scooters while his car was stuck in heavy traffic, and decided to avoid rush hour.

But when he got to the garage where Father Pietro kept his car, Roberto found out that there would be no car chase after all. Someone had parked blocking the garage.

Father Pietro had painted "No parking— access required day and night" on the garage's metal shutters several times, first in white, then in red paint, each time bigger, but it had made no difference. Even when he paid for an official driveway permit and stuck the sign with the permit number on the wall, it didn't make any difference.

It was always the same car blocking the driveway, a white Fiat Punto. Roberto had never seen the driver so had never been able to complain in person. All he had been able to do was leave polite notices under the windscreen wipers.

Unwilling to wait for the owner to turn up and remove the car, Roberto resigned himself to going to the bank on foot.

He walked at a very brisk pace, wishing he had put the envelope in a plastic bag instead of a sock because it was becoming damp with sweat.

When he eventually reached the bank, he felt like a sailor who had finally reached land.

***

Before anything else, Roberto asked for the customers' toilet so that he could retrieve the money without undressing in public. Then he queued nervously for the till.

The bank teller took the envelope, pulled out the notes and fed them through the money counting machine. She ran them through again and announced the amount out loud.

Roberto nodded, despite still struggling to believe how much money it was. He thought about the church's leaky roof, the children's holiday camp, the soup kitchen and all the wonderful things that money could help with. What a marvellous Christmas present for the parish!

"I must ask you about the provenance of this money—it's part of the anti-money-laundering regulation," the teller said.

"A Christmas donation," Roberto replied.

The woman typed something onto her computer, looked at the screen and frowned. "Who made this donation?"

"I have no idea. The envelope was left by our donation box."

She looked at him, then at the money again and frowned a little more.

Roberto sensed that something was wrong.

"Excuse me a moment." She took the notes with her and disappeared into the back of the office.

Was the money fake? Who would give a donation of fake money? What a cruel and senseless thing: they might as well give nothing at all.

Roberto thought of the church roof repairs, the soup kitchen, the children's holiday camp and bid them a sad goodbye.

The sound of sirens intruded into his thoughts. He imagined the police rushing to arrest the person who had forged money in order to give false hopes to innocent people. No, they couldn't have already found the forger. It was probably the police escort for a judge or a politician.

The bank teller still hadn't returned. The noise of the sirens grew nearer. It stopped.

A moment later, four policemen burst into the bank. Maybe they really were coming for the forger!

The teller reappeared and pointed the officers towards Roberto. What was going on?

Before Roberto had had a chance to recalibrate his position from victim to accused, handcuffs had clicked shut on his wrists.

"Excuse me?"

"You're under arrest on suspicion of robbery," the police officer told him.

"Wait. I don't know anything about this!"

"The serial numbers of the banknotes you've just handed in match those of the notes stolen in transit from the mint. Unless you can tell us who gave you this money, you're under suspicion of robbery."

"I don't know who left this money. I found it by the donations box," Roberto repeated.

"You will tell us everything at the police station."

Roberto felt his cheeks flame with embarrassment. The bank's staff, the customers and even a customer's dog— everyone was looking at him. If only he hadn't agreed to take the money to the bank!

***

At the police station, Roberto was questioned for the rest of the morning. Father Pietro was questioned too, but he wasn't charged. Roberto, instead, was charged with robbery, handling stolen goods and money laundering. He was released but forbidden from leaving Palermo until the trial.

"I'm very sorry about this, Roberto," Father Pietro told him as they trudged home together.

"It's not your fault."

"But I asked you to go," Father Pietro said regretfully. "I should have been alerted by the fact that the notes were brand new and in series order—clearly straight out of the mint."

"That doesn't have to mean that they're stolen," Roberto said. "Anyway, who would steal money just to give it away? It makes no sense."

"Maybe they didn't mean to give away," Father Pietro said.

They stopped at a traffic light, waiting to cross.

"You're right. I only noticed the envelope when I lifted the crib's valance. I assumed that it had slipped there after someone missed the slot of the donations' box. But now I think about it, it could just as well have been hidden there on purpose."

On the other side of the road, a mother was a handing a child dripping with melted ice cream to his father.

"Someone could have hidden it there for someone else to pick it up later. Nobody would suspect a church being used as a dead drop."

"I've lost you. Why are we talking about funerals?" Roberto asked.

Father Pietro chuckled. "Not funerals. A dead drop is a mutually agreed place where two spies exchange notes, letters or other items without ever meeting. I read it in spy novels."

The traffic light changed and they crossed.

"Yes, that makes sense, and it would explain last night's break-in: the burglars weren't actually after the paintings—those were just decoys. They were looking for the envelope. Someone was using our nativity scene as a dead drop but I disrupted their plans when I discovered the envelope and took it upstairs."

"Why didn't they break into our house too, then?" Father Pietro asked.

"They probably didn't think that we had found the envelope but believed that the people who should have left the money for them had kept it for themselves instead."

They had almost reached home now.

"That was lucky for us," Father Pietro said, then remembered that Roberto was in trouble because of the money and added, "or maybe it wasn't, actually."

Roberto sighed. "Yes, I wish they had stolen it back. We would have got a fright and a disappointment, but it would have been worth being out of this trouble." He paused. "I'd rather keep this sorry business to ourselves, at least until I've been cleared of all charges, if you don't mind," Roberto said.

"Of course."

They turned the corner and the church came into view. A small crowd was gathered outside it.

"Are we late for Mass?" Roberto checked his watch.

"No. I fear the news has already got here."

"Father Roberto!" one of the boys called him with a good-natured smile. "How did you get yourself caught? You must be more careful. Never mind, even the best get caught sometimes. Welcome to the club."

"But I haven't done anything!" Roberto protested.

"Everyone says that," a woman said. "But don't worry: if the police ask us, we won't say anything."

"But there isn't anything to say. I'm innocent!"

"The most important thing is not to panic, even if they send you to jail. You'll get out eventually," an old man reassured him.

Roberto was mortified. While Father Pietro went in, Roberto remained outside with that small crowd, trying to persuade them of his innocence. When he finally gave up and he went up to the presbytery, he found Father Pietro waiting for him.

"I'm sorry to bring bad news, Roberto. I've just had a call from the bishop. The police have informed him about the charges brought against you. He's convinced of your innocence but he has to suspend you from your duties until you're cleared of all charges."

Roberto felt as if a rock had fallen from the sky and squashed him. "But this is the busiest time of year in the parish!"

"I know, and the bishop knows too. But there are rules to follow and his hands are tied. We'll have to cut down on the Advent activities and cancel some of the Christmas celebrations." Father Pietro sighed. "It's hard, I understand, but try to take this rare chance to have a rest."

Under difference circumstances, Roberto would have rejoiced at the prospect of a rest.

Roberto plonked himself onto the nearest chair. Did his humiliation have no boundaries?

"If I can't help in the parish, I might as well go and stay with my parents and lick my wounds in private." Hopefully, in his hometown, up on the Madonie mountains, people might have not heard of his disgrace.

Father Pietro looked uneasily at his feet.

"Oh no, don't tell me there's more," Roberto groaned.

"You're not allowed to leave Palermo, remember? If your parents want to see you for Christmas, they'll have to come here."

Roberto remembered now. The day had started badly and was getting worse at a catastrophic pace. Roberto retreated to his room and flopped on his bed, feeling sorry for himself. How long would it be before he was tried, proved innocent and reinstated in his job? Meanwhile, his name would be tainted forever. He would have to run away and start anew at the church's equivalent of the French Foreign Legion—the foreign missions, perhaps?

After a bit of moping and a lot of praying, he came to accept his lot. After all, juries, trials and jail had been the main staple of saints and martyrs since the beginning. Hadn't Jesus himself been unjustly accused, unfairly tried, and cruelly executed? Thankfully, there was no capital punishment in Italy anymore, but even if it came to the worst, Roberto would be in very illustrious company.

Having regained his dignity—at least in his mind—and some optimism, Roberto started planning. How could he make good use of all this spare time he had been granted?

If he couldn't assist Father Pietro in the parish duties, he could at least relieve him of the domestic chores. But that would still leave Roberto plenty of spare time. Then, inspiration struck: he would use this time to find the real culprit of the robbery and clear his name.

***

The church's CCTV was the most obvious place to start. Before handing it over to the police, Roberto watched the footage of the burglary. Three men had come within view of the camera but they all wore black clothes and a balaclava that made them impossible to recognise.

They carefully checked the area around the nativity scene, in particular around the donation box and under the valance, then pulled the two paintings off the walls and ran off with them. Roberto had no doubt that they were looking for the envelope.

Next, he watched the footage of the nativity scene. Whoever had left the envelope there must have been caught on camera. Thankfully, the installation had only been set up the morning before Roberto had discovered the envelope, so there were only a few hours of footage to watch.

Roberto got a glass of water and sat patiently in front of the screen. He recognised most of the people who had come to admire the installation. For the ones he couldn't recognise, he called in Father Pietro and, between the two of them, they identified everyone except two sets of tourists.

Roberto assumed that the tourists were unlikely to be involved in the robbery. He might be cutting a corner there, but he imagined that anyone coming on a holiday would want to relax, not undergo the stresses of a robbery. Also, from a practical point of view, it would be nearly impossible to track them down and interview them.

So he made a list of everyone who had come to see the nativity scene, except the tourists, and watched the footage again. He struck off the names of those who hadn't got close enough to the valance sheet to drop the envelope. Four people remained.

Roberto decided he would interview them.

***

Signora Marino was a short and wiry woman who had worn black since her husband's passing, many years ago. The CCTV footage showed that, during her visit to the nativity scene, she had picked up the figurine of the cobbler, had kissed it on the head, and put it back in its workshop. To do this, she had had to get very close to the installation, right by the place where Roberto had found the envelope. This made her a suspect.

Roberto rang the doorbell of her block of flats and, a few moments later, Signora Marino popped her head out of a first-floor window.

At the sight of her sweet, innocent face, Roberto felt that he was wasting his time. But there was no point in having an investigation plan and not sticking to it.

"Hello, Signora Marino. I've come to bring you the Christmas schedule of services," he announced.

It was the excuse he had prepared to start a conversation that would, hopefully, help him find out more about his suspects and decide who was most likely to have abandoned the envelope.

"Thank you. I'll come down."

Roberto heard the sound of hard soles on the stone stairs, the clunking of the door lock, then Signora Marino appeared. "Thank you," she said with a polite smile, and made to shut the door again.

Roberto panicked. This couldn't be the end of their exchanges!

"Actually, I would like to ask you some questions," he said candidly. He hadn't prepared other excuses.

"What questions?" she asked, alarmed. "I'm

very busy. I'm in the middle of cooking."

"I won't take long. Just one question," he pleaded.

This wasn't what he had planned. He had imagined he would have long conversations with his interviewees, during which he would slowly tease out of them all the information he needed without them being any the wiser.

"Go on, then." She glanced behind her shoulders as if in fear that what she was cooking might jump out of her kitchen and come down the stairs.

"Okay. My question is… er…have you lost anything in church recently?"

"No."

"Near the nativity scene, for example?"

"No. If you're asking whether I left the envelope, it wasn't me."

"How do you know about the envelope?" he asked suspiciously.

"Of course I know. Everyone in this neighbourhood knows that you've found an envelope full of stolen money and now you're in trouble with the police."

Roberto was speechless. Signora Marino wasn't the gossipy type. If even she knew, then it was true that everyone did. He felt his cheeks warm. Not only did Signora Marino know about his disgrace, like everyone else, but now she also knew that he suspected her of robbery.

"I'm sorry—"

"It's okay. But I must go back to the hobs. Good luck."

***

Next on Roberto's list were the Obuasi family.

The CCTV showed mum and dad holding their two girls in their arms to show them the nativity scene, while their older brother pushed a toy car back and forth on the stone floor. At one point, the boy's car zipped under the valance and the boy crawled under the fabric to retrieve it.

It looked like a perfectly innocent gesture but Roberto didn't want to leave any stone unturned. The angle of the CCTV camera was such that Roberto couldn't see what the boy was holding, so there was a possibility of him posting an envelope under the valance without being seen by the camera. The robbers could have given the envelope to the boy and instructed him to push it under the valance, even without the parents' consent or knowledge.

This time, though, Roberto had prepared his interview better. He would start with the Christmas services schedule, then he would enquire about how the family was settling— they had recently moved to the neighbourhood and, perhaps, to the country. If circuitous enquiries didn't uncover anything that incriminated or acquitted them, he would ask them plainly: had any of them received an envelope and dropped it under the valance sheet?

With this plan in mind, he set off for their home.

They lived in a ground floor flat not far from Signora Marino's. Delicious smells of exotic cooking wafted out of the French doors into the street. Roberto realised that it would be suppertime soon. Maybe this wasn't a good time for visiting. He was deliberating whether he should return later, when the boy's head peeked out of the window.

"Hello! Have you come to see us?"

"Well…yes, but perhaps your parents are busy."

"No, they're not busy. Mummy is cooking and Daddy is repairing the sink."

Roberto wondered what more they had to be doing to be counted as busy. Maybe these same things but while holding their daughters?

"Perhaps I should come back later," he said.

Just then, Signor Obuasi appeared holding a spanner in one hand and his daughter in the other. Roberto thought that maybe he had been repairing the sink while holding his child!

"Who are you talking to?" he asked the boy, then saw Roberto at the window. "Hello Father! Please, come in."

"I'll come back another time, if you're busy."

"Not at all." He put down the spanner, kept the girl, and strode to the French doors to let Roberto in.

The room was furnished with cushions and throws in vibrant hues and intricate geometric patterns. A map of Ghana hung on one of the walls, opposite a large flag of the country. On a little table sat a framed photograph of the late UN Secretary-General and Nobel Peace Prize recipient, Kofi Annan, with a burning candle.

"He came from Ghana," Mr Obuasi informed Roberto when he saw him looking at the little altar.

This made for a natural topic of conversation, and Roberto and his host talked about their hero until Signora Obuasi appeared with a tray of food.

"Hello, Father. I've made some kelewele for you," she said.

Her son must have informed her of his visit.

Roberto felt very guilty. These kind people were being very hospitable to him and had no idea of the real reason of his visit.

Roberto stood up. "Actually, I should be

going. I just came to give you the schedule of the Christmas services."

"You can't leave without trying my wife's kelewele. She's a very good cook," his host insisted.

Roberto had no choice but stay. The kelewele was a traditional dish of spiced deep-fried plantain. Roberto greatly enjoyed it.

The full supper followed, with jollof rice with fried fish and mixed vegetables.

Roberto's conviction that the Obuasis were completely innocent grew with every mouthful. But there was still a chance that the criminals had used their boy to hide the envelope under the valance. Roberto decided that the best, most honest course of action was to speak clearly to them.

When everyone had finished the main course, Roberto spoke up.

"The Christmas services schedule is only one of the reasons for my visit. There's another matter too." Roberto took a deep breath. "I'm sure you'll have heard about my trouble with some stolen money."

They nodded.

"Yes, Father, but we believe that you're innocent. If there's anything we can do to help you, we'd be happy to," Signor Obuasi said.

"Thank you. Yes, I do need your help. Can

we talk in private?"

The children were sent to play in their rooms. When the adults were alone, Roberto continued.

"I've examined all the CCTV footage around the nativity scene, where I found the envelope behind the valance. The video shows that, when you came to see the installation, your boy—"

"Kofi," the father said.

Of course, Roberto thought.

"—Kofi played with his car on the floor and temporarily disappeared behind the valance."

Roberto examined their facial reactions carefully as he said these words and noticed that the mother's eyebrows twitched with alarm before she quickly recomposed herself. Maybe she knew something.

"Do you think that there could be a chance that someone had given Kofi the envelope with the stolen money and asked him to leave it behind the valance?" Roberto asked.

"No. He would have told us," Signora Obuasi said with complete confidence.

"What makes you so sure? Could he not have told you because he didn't think it was important?"

"No, Father." She looked down. "I know he would have told me because he told me

27

something."

"What did he tell you?"

Signora Obuasi squirmed on her chair. "When he crawled under the nativity scene to retrieve his pullback car, he found a mouse there. But that doesn't mean that you keep the church dirty. It's normal to have mice in old buildings. It doesn't mean that you and Father Pietro don't keep the church clean," she repeated with emphasis.

"Thank you for telling me. It's absolutely fine. Father Pietro and I already knew about a family of mice in the church." He didn't tell her that they had decided not to do anything about them unless they multiplied enough to match the human congregation or chattered as loudly.

But Signora Obuasi still looked uneasy. There must be more to the story.

"Kofi had a sweet in his hand. When he saw the mouse, he gave it to it, and the mouse ran away with it. He shouldn't have fed the vermin, especially as, I'm sure, you and Father Pietro are trying to exterminate them. I'm very sorry about what my boy has done, and I told him off."

"It's fine. I'm sure a sweet won't give the church a mice problem," Roberto said reassuringly, then realised that she probably thought that one mouse already constituted "a mice problem" and corrected himself. "I mean, it won't worsen the problem."

"I'm sure that Kofi would have mentioned the envelope when he told me about the mouse," she concluded.

Roberto agreed. He also imagined that, holding the toy car in one hand and a sweet in the other, the boy didn't have a spare hand to hold an envelope too.

"Thank you. That answers my question… Wait. Who gave Kofi the sweet?"

"I didn't. I don't like my children eating sweets," Signora Obuasi said.

"I didn't either," her husband said.

"The criminals could have bribed him with a sweet and asked him to post the envelope under the nativity scene!" Roberto said.

Kofi was immediately called into the room and questioned.

"I got the sweetie from a man," the boy said simply.

The adults shuddered.

"Do you know his name?" his mum asked.
"No."

"Thank goodness you gave it to the mouse!"

"But you told me off for giving it to the mouse."

"I also told you not to accept sweets from strangers."

"But the teacher said it was okay."

"What teacher?"

Did criminal gangs have designated teachers for young recruits, Roberto wondered.

"My teacher," Kofi said as if everyone was being obtuse. "She took us to the assembly hall, like the rest of the school. The man talked about his books and, when he finished, he gave us sweets as we were leaving to go back to our classrooms."

The man must have been a children books' author visiting the school. Just to make sure, Roberto asked Kofi: "Did the man ask you to do anything for him in exchange?"

"Yes, but I didn't want to. We had to write a story."

Now it was all clear. Roberto thanked Kofi and, when he finally left the Obuasis, he was sure that they had nothing to do with the stolen money.

He had spent a lovely evening in good company and with good food, but he wasn't any closer to finding the truth about the robbery.

Now it was too late to visit to the next people on his list, especially as the Obuasis had given him some food to take home. Father Pietro would enjoy it!

***

Roberto usually liked receiving phone calls from his mum but, that evening, he contemplated the possibility of not answering. He didn't want his mum to know about his disgrace, but how could he keep it from her? She would expect him to visit her, back in his hometown, as soon as the busy Christmas period was over. He had to tell her.

He retreated to his room and picked up the videocall.

He didn't have time to think about how to broach the subject because, as soon as his mum saw him, she asked, "What's wrong?"

So much for him thinking he could keep his problem a secret from her for any length of time! He told her all that had happened and concluded: "I'm sorry but I won't be able to come up and see you until all this is cleared up."

"Don't worry. Your dad and I will come and visit you," she said.

"But you don't like travelling."

The furthest they had ever been from their town was only a few kilometres down the road, and Palermo was more than a hundred kilometres away.

"Don't worry. We'll be fine. There's nothing parents wouldn't do for their children."

***

Now that Roberto knew that his parents would undergo that journey if he couldn't visit them, the urgency to clear his name increased. The next day, Roberto immediately got onto the job of interviewing the next suspect.

Roberto had immediately recognised Tano on the CCTV footage because the teen always hung out with his friends in the square in front of the church. Every afternoon, the youngsters parked their scooters in a circle and sat on them, chatting, scowling at passers-by, wolf-whistling at girls.

The CCTV footage showed the youngsters walking into the church and swarming around the nativity scene. Some dipped their fingers into the miniature stream, others pulled out some moss and threw it at each other, others just stood there and admired the twinkling lights with children's awe.

Out of the group, only Tano had got close enough to the nativity scene to make him a suspect. And he had done so in order to pocket one of the sheep figurines.

That afternoon, Roberto found Tano in the square with his friends as usual.

If finding him wasn't difficult, getting him away from the others to speak to him in private seemed impossible.

Tano was a strong-looking young man and

Roberto had an idea. He walked over to the group and greeted them.

"Hello guys. Tano, I need a strong man to help me move a desk in the parish office."

Instead of being flattered by the compliment, Tano recoiled. "Why me? He's stronger," he replied, volunteering a friend. "Or him. And he's strong too," he said, pointing to another.

"You know what Father wants, Tano," the others mocked him, and some of them started bleating like sheep.

Roberto remembered the sheep figurine and understood. "You're not in trouble," he reassured Tano.

"Then why me?"

The whole group had turned into a bleating herd now. There was so much noise that Roberto couldn't explain anything even if he wanted to.

"Come with me and find out."

Curiosity won over fear and Tano followed Roberto up to the parish office.

"I didn't do anything wrong," Tano said as soon as they were alone.

"Except you stole a sheep from the nativity scene," Roberto said.

"It wasn't for me. It was for my Nonna. She lost one and she needed one more to make four again."

"Why did she need four sheep?"

"Because she has four grandkids. Every sheep means one of us. My cousin said that the missing sheep was me, that it had run away because I'm a black sheep. So I took the sheep from the church because it wasn't black and it was in the church, so it must be at least a bit holy. I dipped it in holy water on the way out too, just to make sure it would be a good sheep. You can't ask for it back because it belongs to my nonna now."

Sympathy swelled in Roberto's heart. After the recent events, Roberto knew what it felt like to be a black sheep.

"Have you found out how your nonna's sheep has gone missing?" he asked Tano.

"It's just lost."

"If I were you, I would enquire with your cousin," Roberto suggested.

Tano looked surprised for a moment, then something clicked in his brain. "You're right! She could have taken it to wind me up!"

"But the sheep is not what I wanted to talk to you about. Do you know anything about an envelope dropped near the donations box?"

"No, Father. I didn't see any envelope when I was there."

Roberto felt that this was enough. If Tano

had known anything about it, Roberto was sure that he wouldn't have been able to hide it.

"That's all, then. Thank you."

Tano returned to his friends and Roberto was satisfied that he was innocent—about the envelope at least.

***

His next suspect was Noemi. The young mother had come into the church with her toddler and had manoeuvred her pushchair really close to the nativity scene. Then she had bent down between the pushchair and the valance. It was quite possible that she had retrieved the envelope from the pushchair's undercarriage and dropped it behind the valance.

Her previous boyfriend—the father of the child—was serving a prison sentence, and her new boyfriend didn't seem to be any more respectable than the previous, Roberto thought. Then he was immediately sorry for the uncharitable thought. Of all people, he was the last who should look down on men who had had run-ins with the law.

Father Pietro had told him that Noemi liked to attend the church's parent-and-toddler group.

Today was their Christmas get-together and Roberto hoped she would be there.

He decided against asking direct questions. A guilty person would be unlikely to admit to their deed and an innocent one would feel unjustly accused. Roberto knew what this felt like and he didn't want to inflict it on anyone else.

So he got himself some work to do, folding and stapling the Christmas service booklets on a table just outside the door of the parent-and-toddler group's meeting room.

He had noticed on previous occasions that many of them gathered outside the door long before the start of their meetings and chatted. With some luck, Noemi would be there and Roberto could overhear her conversations and gather some intelligence.

But when he got there with his box of printouts and his stapler, he found the doors of the meeting room open and some parents and toddlers already inside, preparing the room.

One of the mums saw him. "Father, you are taller than us. Could you put up the bunting and the tinsel? We don't want to get the ladder out with our children around."

This wasn't in the plan, but how could he refuse? Roberto left his box by the door and got to work. After the tinsel and the bunting, he was asked to put up balloons and baubles. Then there were tables to move, chairs to be put out, boxes to carry. When he had finished, the party started and other parents came in with their toddlers. They assumed that he was there to help, and more requests flooded in.

"Could you lay out the pizzette and *arancine*?" one asked. "The crisps bowls need replenishing," another one informed him.

Roberto could see Noemi helping at the soft drinks table but he was rushed off his feet and couldn't get near her.

Despite being in the same room as his suspect, the chances of studying her were very slim. All he managed to find out about her, just from occasional glances, was that she was fond of arancine. Her plate was full of the fried balls of rice and nothing else.

When the party eventually ended, Roberto had been around his suspect for hours but hadn't overheard even a snippet of dialogue or gleaned any useful information.

The printouts of the order of the Christmas Mass, which he had meant to fold and staple, lay scattered on the floor with crayon markings, having been mistaken by the toddlers for colouring paper.

His detective mission had been a complete failure, he thought despondently. He wasn't a good detective, even by the most generous measures. He was only trained to work as a priest. Unfortunately, until he found the real culprits of the mint van robbery, he wasn't going to be allowed to do that.

As he was still there, he was asked to take down the decorations and help put away the tables and chairs.

As he turned one of the tables over to fold it, his fingers landed on something squishy, sticky and still warm. It was recently spat out chewing gum. Yuk!

It must be dangerous to give chewing gums to toddlers. Unless it had been a parent who had stuck it under the table.

He looked around. Noemi was chewing on something in the energetic way people chew on chewing gum rather than food. Roberto had an idea.

With a napkin, he took one *arancina* out of the tray of leftovers and walked up to Noemi.

"Someone ought to eat this last arancina. It's not worth keeping just one," he bluffed, offering it to her.

As Roberto had expected, her face lit up. "Oh yes, please. I'll sacrifice myself," she said.

Before taking the arancina in the napkin, she pulled the chewing gum out of her mouth and stuck it on the underside of the table next to her.

Roberto smiled to himself. He now knew

that she was the culprit of the chewing gum crime but was innocent of the stolen money.

***

Roberto still hadn't touched his supper when Father Pietro had finished his, so busy was he recounting what he had discovered.

"You see, she could have easily used the napkin I was offering her with the arancina. Instead, she stuck her chewing gum under the table. This means that it's an entrenched habit of hers. I've checked the underside of the nativity scene's frame. Sure enough, there's chewing gum stuck just where the CCTV shows Noemi lifting the valance and bending down. She wasn't dropping the envelope with the money after all. She was just discarding her chewing gum. So, I'm back to square one. I have no idea who did it."

"I'm sorry. Is there anything I can do to help?" Father Pietro asked.

"You're already working so hard, running the parish on your own at this very busy time of year. I'm the one feeling sorry because I can't do anything to help you."

"Don't worry about me. Priests don't often get time off so try to make the most of this time of inactivity by resting and relaxing."

But Roberto couldn't rest or relax. Even as he prayed, meditated and read the most interesting books, his mind always went back to the envelope and how he could find the real culprits, clear his name and return to his duties.

The next day, he learnt that one of the parents had complained about him being "invited" to the parent-and-toddler Christmas party.

Roberto immediately thought that the complaint related to the fact that he was being investigated. He later found out that it didn't: the complainant had not been invited after falling out with the party organiser, and had thought it unfair that a non-parent had been invited instead.

Still, Roberto felt uneasy about being seen around the parish. So, as soon as he had finished any housework or other useful activity he could do in the presbytery, he decided to go for a stroll so as not to give offence to anyone and to forget about his troubles.

As he left the church's building, he met the group of boys in the square. Tano saw him and greeted him. "Hello, Father!"

"Hello, Tano," Roberto replied.

"You look down," the boy said. "Don't be. Nobody is cross with you. You weren't stealing for yourself. You were stealing for the parish— for a good cause—like Robin Hood," he said.

Roberto stopped in his tracks. "Do you

really think that I stole the money for the parish?"

"Of course. Everybody does. You've been up to dodgy stuff to get money for the church roof and the police caught up with you. You should have prayed to God to help you get away with it. I'm sure He'd have done it."

"No, that's all wrong. I found the money near the donation box! I had no idea where it came from!"

One of the other boys sucked air through his teeth and shook a hand in the Sicilian gesture for trouble. "You would have been in so much trouble if you'd kept the money. You're lucky the police caught you."

A discussion ensued among the boys about what the criminals would have done to Roberto if they thought he still had the money and was hiding it from them. Roberto wished he wasn't there to hear it. He had gone on a stroll to distract himself from his troubles and this was nothing like that, so he said goodbye to the boys and continued his journey.

Along the way, he met more people, fielded more questions, received more expressions of sympathy. When he finally returned home, he hadn't forgotten about his troubles at all. But he realised that he had got to know his parishioners a lot better. Being relieved from all his duties meant that he could be around them without any hurry or agenda, and give them his time. And they were getting to know him better too.

***

Days went by and, as Roberto was still under travel restrictions, his parents packed their bags, got some tickets and climbed onto a coach to Palermo.

Roberto was sorry for inconveniencing them, and felt that the least he could do was collect them from the coach stop. So he borrowed Father Pietro's car.

When the coach pulled in, his parent waved at him from the window, looking as pleased as sailors who have seen land.

"You look pale and drawn. Have you been eating well?" his mum asked him as soon as she had got him in her arms.

"It's you who look pale and drawn, Mamma," he told her.

His father didn't look better. Both showed the greenish tinge of travel sickness.

"How was your trip?" he asked them both.

"Your mother can't stomach coaches," his father said.

"Don't go telling stories about me. You were even worse, Angelo," his mother retorted.

When they got to the presbytery, to make up

for their ordeals, of which he felt fully responsible, Roberto cooked them a feast.

He prepared a home-made *sfincione* pizza with plenty of onions, anchovies and caciocavallo cheese, the Palermo way, followed by a second course of oven-baked breaded chicken and salad, ending with a traditional Christmas *buccellato* fruitcake for pudding.

This last one was a present from Signora Marino. Since he'd knocked at her door, she had lavished him with gifts. Roberto had concluded that they were apologies for having sent him away so briskly when he visited her. But he could only guess, because he hadn't spoken to her since that day. Her gifts were always delivered by other people and he hadn't seen her in church recently.

Unfortunately, despite the feast laid out in front of them, his parents were still lacking an appetite. They picked at their food like sparrows, then excused themselves to their room for a long afternoon siesta. Roberto had prepared the presbytery's spare room for them.

At least Father Pietro enjoyed Roberto's feast when he arrived home, hungry and tired, after a morning of home visits to the sick and homebound.

"You look sad. Are your parents okay?" Father Pietro asked.

"I feel guilty about them having travelled to see me. And I have no idea how long it will be before I'm released from this nightmare."

Father Pietro put a slice of Signora Marino's buccellato in his mouth and sighed. Roberto wondered whether it was a sigh of sympathy for him or of culinary appreciation for the buccellato.

"Don't worry about your parents. A bit of travelling won't harm them. In fact, once they get used to it, they might even start to enjoy it. And I expect that they're happy to see your home, your parish and your community, and celebrate Christmas with you. Afterall, parents would do anything for their children."

***

Christmas Eve finally arrived. Roberto resolved to put all his woes into God's hands and forget about them until the festivities were over.

The midnight Mass was so well attended that there was standing room only. It had been a long time since Roberto had been to a Mass without celebrating it, and even longer since he had sat in a pew with his parents.

Thanks to his hatch, he had successfully installed Baby Jesus in his crib without any damage to the rest of Bethlehem, and at the end of the service, a small crowd gathered to admire the nativity scene, including his parents.

"It's so beautiful. So detailed, so many different crafts and trades... and even real running water!" his mother said.

She stretched her hand towards it and, for a moment, Roberto feared she might dip her fingers in the stream and give a bad example to other bystanders. Instead, she straightened one of the shepherds who was balancing precariously over a ravine, possibly knocked out of place by Roberto when he had shaken the structure to open the crib's hatch.

That gesture of his mother gave Roberto a moment of déjà vu. Another woman had stretched her arm towards the nativity scene and touched one of the statuettes. He remembered it from the CCTV footage he had studied. But who?

Suddenly, he remembered. And someone else had done it too! His heart beat faster. He might have found who had dropped the envelope and who had robbed the mint van!

"I've got to do something urgently. Can I leave you and see you at home?"

"Of course," his parents said. The presbytery was only on the top floor of the building attached to the church.

Roberto rushed to the parish office and retrieved the CCTV footage. Just as he remembered, Signora Marino had picked up the cobbler's figurine from the nativity scene and had kissed his head before putting him back in his workshop. Roberto fast forwarded to the night of the burglary. One of the burglars too had picked the cobbler and kissed him.

There must be a link between Signora Marino and the burglar. Signora Marino's late husband was a cobbler. She had kissed the cobbler's figurine remembering her husband. The burglar had done the same, remembering... his father?

Signora Marino looked so innocent that he hadn't pursued her lead. But his own mum's words and Father Pietro's echoed in his head: parents would do almost anything for their children. Including, sometimes, the wrong thing.

This would explain why she was lavishing Roberto with gifts: she must feel guilty about landing him into trouble with the police.

Father Pietro came in. "There you are. I was looking for you everywhere."

"I think I've found the culprits."

"Wow. What a great Christmas present for us!"

Roberto showed Pietro the footage and explained his theory. "Gero and his accomplices robbed the mint van and hid various portions of the loot in several places. One of them was at his mum's. When he felt the time was right, he asked her to hand it over using the nativity scene as a dead drop. He would have collected it that night, when he broke into the church. But I disrupted their plan by discovering it and taking it upstairs."

***

The day after Boxing Day, Roberto went to the police and told them his theory, with all the reasons and proofs. The man in the CCTV footage matched Gero's frame and, after questioning, the young man confessed to the robbery. He had persuaded his mother to hide the money until the case had grown cold. Then he had asked his mum to hide it under the nativity scene. In all this, Signora Marino had been reluctant to help, all the time wishing her son would turn away from his criminal ways. But her fear of him going to jail had prevailed and she had agreed to hide the money for him.

He agreed to cooperate with the police in exchange for his mother not being charged. He promised her that he would study in prison and turn a new leaf.

Roberto was cleared of all charges and was reinstated in his duties in the parish.

"I knew you would be cleared quickly.

Nobody could seriously believe that you're a criminal," his mum told him.

"If you thought that it would be over quickly, why didn't you just wait for me to visit you, instead of coming here?" Roberto asked.

She smiled. "It was time your father and I visited you. We've always wondered what your parish looked like."

Father Pietro had been right. Roberto felt a lot better.

***

The following day, Signora Marino rang the presbytery's doorbell.

Roberto braced himself for a confrontation. She might have felt sorry for him when he was going to stand trial in place of her son, but now that her son was going behind bars thanks to Roberto, her feelings towards him might have changed. Roberto took a deep breath and opened the door.

Signora Marino smiled. "Hello, Father. I've come to thank you." She handed him a cake-shaped parcel.

Roberto was confused. "What for?"

"Two things: the first is that you've done what I wasn't brave enough to do. I should have handed my son over to the police earlier. He's turned a corner now and I'm confident that they will help him change his life. The second thing is that you didn't go to the police as soon as you realised that it was us. Instead, you allowed us to spend Christmas together. It'll be our last one together for a while. Thank you."

**

Roberto's parents stayed until the New Year, then went home. Roberto resumed his parish duties. Normality had never felt so good.

Now Roberto and Father Pietro were getting ready to visit the bishop and discuss funding for the church's roof repair.

"If the money in that envelope had been a real donation, our fundraising would be over by now," Roberto said wryly.

"Not necessarily. The parish council might have decided to use the funds for something else," Father Pietro said with a wink.

Roberto smiled as he remembered their earlier disagreements on the topic. "I'm going to say something controversial but, in a way, I'm glad we don't have that money. It caused trouble from the moment it landed in our hands."

"You have a point. But let's first see if the bishop can help us or not."

The bishop's curia was far and they decided to take the car. They headed down to the garage in plenty of time, in case the white Fiat

Punto was blocking the garage's exit as usual.

But this time there was no sign of the car. The exit was completely clear, and the road was wet with rain throughout, showing that no car had been parked there for a while.

Roberto and Pietro were pulling up the roller shutters when Tano rode past on his scooter and stopped.

"Hello, Fathers. It's nice not to have your garage blocked anymore, isn't it?" he said.

Roberto had no idea that their struggles had been noticed. "Yes, we're lucky today."

"Not just today. You won't have that problem again—at least, for some time," Tano said.

"How can you tell?"

"The owner of that car is in jail now," Tano said, revving his engine with satisfaction.

"You knew whose car it was?"

"Everyone knew except you. But you couldn't have done anything about it anyway. He wasn't someone you wanted to mess with."

"Whose car was it, then?"

"Gero Marino's, of course."

Roberto chuckled. Sometimes, mysteries were simpler to solve than one had imagined.

"Have a good day, Fathers," Tano said.

"And you, Tano," Roberto replied, and watched Tano roar off on his scooter.

He felt a warmth in his heart for the young man. The black sheep actually had a very kind heart.

So did most of his parishioners, despite all their faults and foibles. Yes, Roberto thought, he loved his parish—even when his parishioners went overboard with the nativity scene, stuck chewing gum to the underside of tables, or protected their criminal children.

As he set off with Father Pietro to ask the bishop for the money for the roof, Roberto knew that he was where he ought to be, doing what he ought to be doing.

2. THE MISSING MONEY

Father Roberto felt a pang of panic as the minibus drove off and left him alone. Actually, the problem was that he wasn't alone: he was in charge of twenty-four children until Mrs Grassi returned from parking the minibus.

No philosophical theory, no theological insight, no liturgical training in the seminary had prepared him for this. He searched his memory, but none of the books he'd studied answered the question: how do you take more seven- and eight-year-olds than you've got hands for safely across a Palermo road?

Or, if you decide to keep the excited lot on the pavement until help arrives, how can you stop them from spilling onto the road like marbles?

"Father Roberto, what are we waiting for?"

one of the children asked.

"We're waiting for Mrs Grassi to park the minibus and rejoin us."

"But she said, 'Go ahead without me'. I heard her. Look, the theatre is just there! Let's go!"

"No, we must wait for Mrs Grassi."

"There she is!" another child announced.

"It's very kind, but you didn't have to wait for me," Mrs Grassi said, waddling over.

"Not a problem at all," Roberto replied sincerely.

"Right, children, line up two by two behind me. Hold hands. No pushing! Matteo, go to the back of the queue! Father will stop the traffic and we'll cross the road."

Before Roberto had time to worry about how he'd stop the torrent of cars and scooters, the children formed a human millipede like a well-rehearsed platoon, and cars and scooters immediately slowed down.

On the façade of the theatre hung puppets in shiny armour, wielding embossed brass shields, with deep red and green velvet skirts and flamboyant feathers cascading down their helmets.

"Father Roberto, have you taken us here because it's about the Crusades?" a little girl asked, pointing to a puppet in a Crusader's outfit.

"Certainly not! These puppets are a traditional Sicilian –

"I've studied the Crusades in school!" a boy interrupted, brandishing an imaginary sword. "Have you been in the Crusades, Father Roberto?"

"Father, would you like to get the tickets?" Mrs Grassi cut in.

"Of course, of course," he replied, glad for the conversation to steer away from a regrettable part of Christianity's history.

He pulled out of his pocket an envelope with Theatre tickets, 145 euros written on it. The money came from a grant Mrs Grassi had obtained from the town mayor. As all their children came from underprivileged families, Mrs Grassi had made a good case for their cause.

Very soon after taking up post in the parish, Roberto had discovered the power of women like Mrs Grassi.

When the children's nativity play looked set to be under-attended (the police had recently raided the area and taken to jail many of their family members), Mrs Grassi roped in all the parish confraternities, prayer groups and associations until there was a full house.

When the pest control people insisted that

they'd completely cleared the sacristy of rats, she mailed them the cadavers of the rats she'd poisoned after their visit and they returned to finish the job, free of charge.

"One hundred and forty-five euros," the ticketing lady announced.

Roberto tore open the envelope and counted twenty, forty, sixty, eighty, one hundred euros. That was all there was? He counted again. There were definitely only one hundred euros.

"I'm sorry, I seem to be missing some of the money."

The old lady quickly pulled the tickets back behind the glass.

"Please, can you check the envelope too?" Roberto asked Mrs Grassi.

She didn't. Instead, she stuck out her chest and addressed the ticketing lady.

"Surely you give group discounts?"

"No discounts, sorry," the old lady replied, stone-faced.

Mrs Grassi's lower lip twitched. It was a sign that she was displeased. Roberto had seen it before, when the kids had been too boisterous.

"We are a church holiday camp and these are poor children. Their parents struggle to feed them," Mrs Grassi said.

"We're struggling too. I cannot give any

discount."

"We haven't got any more money and you don't take credit cards," Mrs Grassi insisted, opening her wallet and showing it to the old lady.

"No discounts."

"We can't take the children back now that they're here and excited!"

Roberto marvelled at Mrs Grasso's ability to instantly switch from angry to pleading.

"It's not my problem."

"Alright, I'll come back tomorrow with the rest of the money," Mrs Grassi said theatrically.

The tinkling music of a barrel organ started playing inside the theatre and the audience clapped. The show must be starting. The ticketing lady fixed Roberto in the eyes.

"No, not you. Him," she said to Mrs Grassi, pointing to Roberto. "If he says that he'll come back tomorrow morning with the rest of the money, I'll let you in."

"Yes, I'll be here tomorrow first thing in the morning!" Roberto replied eagerly, without thinking.

"All right. Hurry in, you're late. The show's already started!"

***

"I'm sure we put aside one hundred and forty-five euros for the theatre tickets. We've written it on the envelope too. Where have the forty-five euros gone?" he wondered aloud, sitting at the table with Mrs Grassi in the empty parish hall.

Nine envelopes, one for each of the remaining days of the camp, lay open on the table. Every envelope contained exactly the money Roberto and Mrs Grassi had budgeted for that day's activity – not a cent more or less.

"They might have slipped under a chair, fallen behind a cupboard, been swept by a gust of wind, who knows? I'm sure we'll eventually find them, but there's nothing we can do to hasten it."

"But how am I going to pay the lady tomorrow?"

Mrs Grassi arched an eyebrow and threw herself back against the chair. "Are you really thinking of going back to pay her—after she refused to give a group discount to a party of underprivileged children? There's nowhere you don't get a group discount these days!"

"I gave her my word."

"You didn't. You only said 'yes'."

"Hello, hello, hello!" a male voice boomed from the door, and Mr Cavoli strutted in. "I was on my way to Mass and I saw the car of the lovely Signora Grassi outside, so I decided to pop in and say hello."

"Mass is at six and now it's only three o' clock," Mrs Grassi replied dryly.

"Time is never too long in your company, Angela."

"Cut it out, Peppe, we're busy. What do you want?"

"If you're busy, I will help you. What can I do?"

"The only help we need is for somebody to magic forty-five euros out of the air," she said, pushing the hot August air against her face with her lace fan.

He smiled smugly, rummaged in his pockets, pulled out a wad of cash and unfolded a fifty-euro note onto the table. "Here you are. Abracadabra."

"Bravo," Mrs Grassi said sarcastically, "but we need one we can keep."

"You can keep this one."

"Please, let's not joke with money," Roberto said, pushing the note into Mr Cavoli's hands.

"I'm not joking. This is a gift, in honour of the most beautiful woman in Palermo."

"It's not me who needs the money, it's the parish, silly!" she replied, fanning herself with more energy.

"All the same, here, take it," Mr Cavoli insisted, pushing the note back onto the table.

"What are you hoping to get in return?" she asked suspiciously.

"A glimpse of the light of your eyes, or nothing at all. Go on, take it. It's rude to refuse a gift," he said.

By now Roberto was decidedly uncomfortable about this flirtatious banter.

"Mr Cavoli, if you are serious about this gift, I thank you on behalf of the parish. But I wouldn't pursue this damsel any further because she's already married, and so are you."

"Ah, Father, I mean no harm! Anyway, her husband's only the shadow of the man he was," Mr Cavoli said, and sauntered off before anyone could reply.

***

Roberto swirled a thread of oil onto the bean soup, thinking about Mr Cavoli's present. Had he been right to accept? It certainly had saved him from defaulting on his promise to the ticketing lady.

He felt a pang of guilt as he admitted to himself that he disliked the man, even after his donation.

Was it because Mr Cavoli flirted with his beloved Mrs Grassi? Maybe it was the way he strutted about the parish as if he owned it.

Father Pietro, the boss, hobbled to the table with one shoeless foot. As diocesan priests, they were under no vow to live, eat or pray together, but still they loved doing all three.

"What happened to you?" Roberto asked.

"Oh, don't worry. I'm just trying to fix my sandal's strap. Every time I glue it back, it breaks again."

"I think you should buy yourself some new sandals," Roberto said, "or go to a cobbler."

"I can fix it. Every cent we save is most welcome," Father Pietro replied, furrowing his forehead. "Today I've had the building surveyors into the church and they confirmed that the leak in the roof is very serious and needs urgent—and costly—repair."

"That's not good news!"

"I was wondering if our formidable Mrs Grassi could be put on the case. She might be able to get us some grant, sponsorship or, if all else fails, a loan. Could you speak to her when you see her?"

"Yes, I will. She might find us some generous donor. By the way, today Mr Cavoli donated fifty euros for the summer camp," Roberto said, and hesitated before continuing. "Paying for the church roof repairs is on another scale, of course. But I wonder, what does Mr Cavoli do for a living? He pulled a large wad of cash out of his pocket. Is he really wealthy?"

"He sells second-hand cars and scooters. We bought our car from him."

"Is it any good?" Roberto asked, even though he realised the question was irrelevant and had been motivated by his distrust of the man.

"It's great. You should get yourself a driving licence, Roberto. It would really help you. I don't know why I'm saying this, because then I'd have to share the car with you. But when someone calls us from the hospital in the middle of the night, and there are no buses…"

"…then you go rather than me!" Roberto said with a chuckle.

"That's exactly the problem!"

***

Without the puppets hanging off the front, the theatre's smog-stained façade looked like the make-up-streaked face of a woman who has partied for too long. The cracks in the carved wood of the large doors were like age wrinkles, the termite holes resembling dirty pores.

Roberto hadn't thought about the possibility of finding it shut. He walked closer. After all, the lady had told him to come "tomorrow morning".

"Are you looking for someone?" a phlegmy voice called through the tilted shutters of a ground-floor window.

"Yes. I've come to settle a debt for some tickets I bought yesterday."

"Peppina!" the old man shouted, then opened the shutters.

In one hand he cradled a freshly cut piece of wood, coarsely shaped like the head of a puppet. In the other hand he held a carving tool.

"My wife is coming. I'm Antonio Cusumano, the last of the Cusumanos, puppeteers since 1827. Come in."

Roberto complied and found himself in the man's workshop. The walls were plastered with puppets at various stages of creation or repair. On the worktop, tools were scattered like dice and a freshly painted wooden head was clamped to dry.

An old woman walked in and Roberto recognised the ticketing lady. She recognised him too, and said to her husband, "I told you that he'd come!"

Roberto quickly pulled out the money from his pocket.

"Thank you for giving us credit and sorry for the trouble," he said, and turned to leave.

"Can I offer you a coffee?"

"Thank you, but now I'm expected back for the kids' camp."

"Come, come, follow me." The woman

beckoned, as if Roberto's answer had been positive.

"Go on, go," the old man instructed him too.

Roberto realised that he'd offend them if he insisted on leaving. So he followed her through a musty and dingy corridor with puppets hanging off the walls like they were picture frames.

He wasn't sure where the workshop ended and the private dwelling started: they blended one into the other like a grafted tree.

A sink and a stove signalled that they'd reached the kitchen. It was crammed full of stuff and felt like an oppressive cave.

Puppets stared silently at Roberto from unexpected places like spying children, and startled him a couple of times. The old lady pulled out a chair, removed the puppet sitting on it, and offered it to Roberto.

"I'm really sorry that we couldn't give you a discount, Father. The rent keeps going up and the number of customers down. Nowadays we mostly get tourists. They come once and that's it. Before there was the TV, Sicilian families came every Saturday and my husband and his father staged a different episode of 'The Furious Orlando' every week. Now he always does the same story, over and over, because each week we have new people."

"So your husband is the puppeteer as well as the puppet-maker?"

"Yes, but I don't know if he'll be able to do the shows for much longer. Manoeuvring a seven-kilogram puppet for one hour solid, saying each puppet's part, shouting and banging their weapons, it's very hard work. Maybe the days of the Cusumano puppet company are numbered."

"You need an apprentice."

"We have no children."

"Has your husband thought of giving workshops? I think that children would love to learn about how puppets are made. He could visit schools and holiday camps, for example. I'm sure our children would love it. In fact, today they'll be making their own puppets with papier-mâché. Why doesn't he try it out on us? Of course, we'll pay him a fee," Roberto said, and immediately regretted it. Where could he possibly find the money to pay them?

But it was too late. The woman's eyes lit up with the confidence of one who knows that her husband is the head of the family but she's the neck which turns the head.

***

When Roberto finally reached the parish, the summer camp had already started and Mrs

Grassi was rushed off her feet.

"I knew you wouldn't make it back from the theatre in time. I hope that at least they were grateful."

"Yes, they were. They really need the money; their business isn't doing at all well," he said, trying to smooth the way for telling her about the workshop he'd promised.

"If we keep giving charity to others, we'll never have enough for ourselves! I don't agree with this workshop," she said when Roberto did tell her.

She had secured the funding for the camp so it was only fair that she should have veto power on the way it was used. Still, Roberto didn't give up.

"But you know how the widow at Zarephath never ran out of food when she shared the little she had with Elijah."

"The Cusumanos are not the prophet Elijah. They're scoundrels."

After more negotiation, Mrs Grassi sighed. "We've planned an activity for each day, so when would we do this workshop?"

"We could have it instead of the beach trip."

Roberto hated sand, salty water and the unforgiving August sun.

"You try telling the children that we're not taking them to the beach! No. We can have the workshop instead of the trip to the sanctuary."

"That's tomorrow. Great."

Then Roberto realised that, as the entry to the sanctuary was free, the money allocated for that day's activities would be just the cost of the minibus's fuel.

It looked like the Cusumanos weren't going to get much for their trouble, but he didn't feel he was in a position to ask anything more.

***

The Cusumanos arrived at the parish hall earlier than expected. An enjoyable morning should be awaiting Roberto, but a black cloud hung over it.

Roberto was acutely aware that the minibus fuel funds weren't enough to thank the Cusumanos for their time. Especially as they had lugged along two suitcases full of material for their workshop.

The children sat down at their tables and watched carefully as the Cusumanos pulled puppets, tools and richly coloured cloths out of their cases.

"That's Angelica! That's Orlando!" they shouted as they recognised the puppets which had starred in the show.

Mr Cusumano looked tenderly and lovingly at his puppets and answered all the children's questions.

Roberto imagined God looking at humans like Mr Cusumano looked at his puppets.

Mrs Grassi seemed to have warmed to the elderly couple: when the Cusumanos invited the children to touch the puppets, Roberto saw her hands reach out too.

"Oh, what a lovely thing! Puppets! It must have been Mrs Grassi's idea," a voice called from the back of the hall. It was Mr Cavoli.

Roberto tensed up. Didn't the man have anything else to do with his time than bothering Mrs Grassi?

"No, it was Father's idea," she snapped, quickly withdrawing her hand from the puppet.

Mrs Cusumano smiled at Mr Cavoli. "Here's a strong man. Would you like to try manoeuvring our puppet?"

That request pricked Roberto's pride— wasn't he a strong-looking man too, and younger than middle-aged Mr Cavoli?

But it must have been just the sort of invitation Mr Cavoli had hoped for. He grabbed the red-feathered knight and brandished his tin sword.

"I'm a knight, and I'll fight anyone, for my Angela!"

"The name is Angelica," Mrs Grassi corrected him.

"No, the name for me is Angela. Who wants

to fight with me?" he replied.

"Me!" the children cried.

Chaos ensued as each child reached for the nearest object vaguely shaped like a sword and attacked the puppet, until Mrs Grassi, red in the face and puffing with anger, confiscated all weapons.

Mr Cavoli performed a theatrical flourish to Mrs Grassi and left, the children settled down at their desks and Roberto breathed a sigh of relief.

The Cusumanos turned out to be even better teachers than they were puppeteers. After their demonstration, they went round helping each child.

Roberto wasn't any good at handiwork, but he sat down next to a girl who was asking for help.

She offered him a thread and a needle. The times Roberto had managed to thread a needle could be counted on the fingers he'd pricked. He tried three time but missed.

"You need to lick and squeeze the thread, that's what my mum does," a boy suggested helpfully.

Roberto recoiled, but the boy stood over him until he had tried, and succeeded.

"Good job!" the boy said to him with genuine enthusiasm.

Roberto felt happy. By the end of the morning, he decided he liked working with children after all.

"Thank you very much for coming today," he said to the old couple at the end of the workshop. He handed them the envelope with the money. "I'm sorry it's not much, but I will give you good publicity online and I will spread the word about your workshops and your shows."

"Thank you, Father."

***

"Hello, Father Roberto?" a voice said down the phone.

Roberto was sitting behind the desk in the parish office, opposite a doe-eyed couple keen to book a wedding date.

"Yes, speaking."

"I'd never have imagined you'd do something like this! You've insulted us! If you didn't want to pay us, why didn't you say so?"

"I don't understand…"

"Did you think that an empty envelope was a clever joke? Well, it's not! It's a vile trick by cowardly people."

It sounded like Mrs Cusumano's voice, spilling out of the phone into the room.

"I don't know what you're talking about."

"Shame on you! You don't deserve to be

called a priest," she said, and cut off the call.

Roberto's bones turned to stone. It sounded as if the envelope he'd given the Cusumanos didn't even contain the fuel money. If it was empty, then somebody was stealing the summer camp money.

He wanted to call Mrs Cusumano back and explain to her. But what? That he suspected there was a thief? A likely story!

The Cusumanos must be paid and Roberto wouldn't call them until he'd got the money to do it.

He put the phone down and looked at the bewildered couple in front of him, forcing an innocent smile.

**

Mrs Cusumano's phone call had distressed him to the point that he'd forgotten the time and stayed in the parish office until well after closing time.

As he padded up the stairs home, he rehearsed how he'd tell Father Pietro about the missing money. He desperately needed his advice.

He was so absorbed in these thoughts that he didn't greet him from the door, as he usually did, but floated silently into the dining room.

Father Pietro was bent over the table, his back to the door.

"Hi," Roberto said.

The priest jumped so high that he was in danger of slipping out of his sandals. He turned around with a flustered look and shifted his body as if to cover the table behind him.

"Is everything all right?" Roberto asked.

"Yes ...Yes!" Father Pietro stammered.

He turned back to face the table and stuffed whatever was on it into his shirt's top pocket. As he turned around to leave, a ten-euro note glided to the floor.

"You've lost this," Roberto said, picking it up.

"Oh, yes, yes… Thank you."

He took the note from Roberto's hand, avoiding his gaze.

"What are you up to?" Roberto asked as nonchalantly as he could.

But Father Pietro scuttled off without answering.

Father Pietro wasn't a secretive person. Roberto didn't like what had just happened and decided that he wouldn't share his story with him either.

***

Roberto disliked the sand, the glare of the sun and the stickiness of sun cream. Also he knew that, being a man, he was expected to play rough and tumble with the boys.

Many of them hadn't seen their jailed fathers for a long time, and some didn't even know who their fathers were.

It's hard to imagine God as a loving father if you've never experienced one, Roberto thought, so he was determined to be as fatherly as he could. But how to connect with the boys when he couldn't kick a ball straight or run on the sand without tripping over?

With these thoughts in his head, plus a burning desire to tell Mrs Grassi about the Cusumanos' empty envelope, and the duty to pass on to her Father Pietro's request about the roof repairs, Roberto set off to unlock the hall.

The kids were already outside—towels around their necks, flip-flops on their feet. Roberto sighed as he realised that there was no way he'd catch Mrs Grassi alone before the trip.

When they got to the beach, the children were so fascinated with the texture of the sand that they didn't want to do anything other than handle this magical stuff.

Roberto then discovered that many of them had never been to the sea, even though they lived in a coastal city. So he suggested they should make a sand castle. Soon a massive construction site began, buzzing with activity.

"The bastions here! The moat there! More

water! More sand!" Roberto instructed, until they had created the most magnificent set of mediaeval fortifications that beach had ever seen.

Maybe the dazzling sunshine and the roasting sand were not half as bad as he thought, so long as one was in pleasant company, and he had come to the conclusion that children's company was the best ever.

At midday, though, Roberto had to retreat under the sun umbrella. His skin was sore as he had stupidly removed his shirt and had been too shy to ask Mrs Grassi to spread sun lotion on his back.

"Thank you for bringing a beach umbrella!" he said to Mrs Grassi, as she sat next to him, her brow sweaty.

"By the way, thinking about shelter, I've remembered that Father Pietro told me to ask you something. The church's roof leaks and we need to repair it urgently. Of course, we haven't got any money. Do you think you could get on the case and see if you can find a grant, or a sponsorship or a donation?"

"Why didn't Father Pietro come and ask me himself?"

"He knows that I see you every day, I suppose."

"Still, he could have bothered himself."

Roberto looked at her to check if she was joking. He'd never heard Mrs Grassi say a bad word about Father Pietro. Yes, she could be a bit sharp about people, but she'd never hinted a dislike for her parish priest. Was Father Pietro up to something she disapproved of?

"What makes you say that?" he enquired.

She didn't reply, but stood up and shouted. "Children, sit in a circle for your ice cream!"

The kids rushed to the call and obediently sat in a circle on the hot sand.

The moment of confidences had passed. Roberto pushed all his unpleasant thoughts out of his mind and decided to enjoy the ice cream.

Mrs Grassi opened a cold bag full of ice creams and lollies. It looked just like a pirate's treasure chest washed up on a beach.

"I thought we were going to the ice cream kiosk," one of the children said.

"No, I bought them from the supermarket, which is cheaper."

"Don't tell me today's envelope money has disappeared too!" Roberto whispered to her.

She looked surprised. "Well, actually, yes. How do you know?"

He sighed. "The envelope I gave the Cusumanos was empty."

She gave him a sympathetic look. "Try not to think about it and enjoy the rest of this trip."

Drunk with sunshine, fun and sea waves, the children fell asleep in the minibus on the way home. Mrs Grassi drove carefully and smoothly, as usual, and Roberto felt sleepy too. But questions crowded his mind.

"What do you think happened to the money?" he asked her.

"I don't know. Every evening now I check all the envelopes, and the money's all there. Then, in the morning, something's missing."

"Who's got keys to the parish hall?"

"You, me and Father Pietro. He keeps them in a cabinet in the sacristy."

A horrible thought swept Roberto's mind, connecting Father Pietro's shifty behaviour the night before, the banknote dropping off the table, and Mrs Grassi's earlier sharpness about him. Roberto pushed the horrid suspicion out of his head like a sin.

"Do you think that someone could take the keys away briefly and put them back without anyone noticing?" he asked.

"I guess they could even copy them and put them back without anyone noticing. But only if they're people who usually help out in the sacristy."

Mr Cavoli! He always helped at the weekday evening Mass. But he had wads of cash in his pockets. What would make him turn petty thief?

With these thoughts swirling in his mind, Roberto was dropped off at home and was about to close the door onto the street when he noticed a young man standing on the pavement opposite the church, shiftily looking left and right. The rumble of a scooter made the man look in the direction of the noise. Oh, no, had the church become a meeting point for illicit deals?

The man glanced at Roberto, who swiftly closed the door but peered through the peep hole. A scooter arrived and stopped by the man. It was Mr Cavoli!

The two men exchanged something and then went off in different directions. Mr Cavoli must be the thief. He was dodgy enough. A traitor in the heart of the flock. That night Roberto didn't sleep well.

***

It was 5.30 pm and it was Roberto's turn to man the confessions booth. On a hot summer's weekday, he didn't think many penitents would turn up, so he took a book about the lives of saints with him.

As he walked down the stairs from the flat to the church, he thought he heard the sound of a barrel organ. He looked out of a little window and saw a gathering just outside the church, so he decided to pop across for a moment.

When he made it to the front of the crowd, a shiver ran down his spine. The Cusumanos had set up an impromptu puppet show on the pavement, right outside his church.

Knowing how Mrs Cusumano had reacted to the empty envelope, and that she believed it to have been a nasty joke, he thought that nothing good could be coming out of this.

"Here's your daughter, whom I rescued from the fire-spitting dragon at the peril of my life," the knight said to the king.

"Good. Here, take your reward," the king replied, and the knight took a treasure chest.

The organ played cheerful music and the knight clanked off stage.

"Ah, ah, ah, I've tricked him! There's no treasure in the chest, it's empty!" the king cackled.

The audience booed.

So this was a parable about him!

"The plot is wrong!" he shouted at the top of his voice.

The organ stopped and everyone turned to look at him. Mr and Mrs Cusumano popped their heads up from behind the stage, scowling.

"The king had absolutely no idea that the

chest was empty! An evil wizard stole the treasure! When the king finds this out, he wants to give a treasure to the knight but he hasn't got any treasure left. He's a poor king. All he possesses is… a book," Roberto said, stepping forward and offering the king puppet his book of saints.

The king puppet took it and the organ started playing again. The knight rumbled onstage, raging with anger, and was immediately appeased by the king's gift of the book. The audience clapped.

Was it peace now, Roberto wondered, and hoped so.

The church bell struck quarter to six. He was a quarter of an hour late for confessions!

He rushed inside the church, opened the creaky hatches of the wooden booth, turned on the little dingy light and sat on the bench polished by decades of his predecessors' cassocked bottoms.

Immediately, somebody knelt at the other side of the window. They must have been waiting for him but too embarrassed to be seen queueing by the confessional.

"Good evening, Father," a man's voice whispered through the metal grating.

Although he couldn't see his face, Roberto recognised Mr Cavoli's deep baritone.

Adrenaline revved up his heart. He was about to find out that Mr Cavoli had stolen from the summer camp envelopes; he had no doubt about it.

Even better, the thefts would stop. Why else would Mr Cavoli come for confession if he wasn't sorry about it and intended to stop?

"Good evening to you. In the name of the Father, and the Son and the Holy Spirit," he said cheerfully.

"I confess to Almighty God and to you, Father, that I have sinned… Father, you are bound to secrecy, aren't you?"

"Of course! Please, go ahead." Roberto's hands turned clammy.

"My wife is an unbearable woman: always nagging, ever demanding, never happy. I've put up with her for so many years, Father. Last night she discovered a letter that I wrote to another woman. She started screaming at me, breaking plates, throwing my stuff out of the window. I begged her not to tell our children and guess what she said?"

"I thought you were coming to confess your sins, not your wife's."

"She said she'll tell our children, and the grandchildren too! Father, I didn't do anything wrong with this other woman. I only sent her love letters."

"Writing love letters to Mrs Gra…ahem, another woman, is definitely cheating on your wife. If you want absolution, you need to be sorry for it and stop it."

"I'm sorry now."

That didn't sound exactly like repentance, Roberto thought, but he was desperate to find out about the thefts, so he moved on.

"Are there other sins you need to confess?"

"Sometimes I've said swear words and sometimes I forget to say my prayers."

An expectant silence followed.

"Are you sure there's nothing else?"

"Pardon?"

"Have you ever stolen anything?"

"Of course not!"

"Are you sure?"

"Oh, I see! You mean, have I paid my taxes—I paid attention to your homily last Sunday, Father!"

"I didn't mean that, but have you?"

"Sometimes, not always. Nobody pays tax if they can avoid it, Father."

Wrong answer, in many ways. Roberto was getting impatient.

"That's something to confess too. But I meant something else. Summer camp envelopes? Does that ring a bell? Plus, weren't you exchanging something with a young man, yesterday evening, in front of the church?"

"Father, you're supposed to at least pretend not to know who I am."

Roberto felt a hot rush of blood to his cheeks. "Sorry... of course."

"I don't know anything about those envelopes, and that man from last night is my nephew. He's got a gambling addiction, so every month he gives me his salary and I give it back to him little by little so that he can't gamble it away."

Whatever Mr Cavoli's marital and tax sins, he wasn't the envelope thief. Roberto felt silly and ashamed.

"Now, Father, can I be absolved?"

"Yes, if you promise there will be no love letters, no flirting, no daydreaming. And, for your penance, you'll go on a marital counselling weekend with your wife. If she doesn't want to go, tell me and I'll speak to her."

"Ah, Father. That's really harsh!"

***

The August air was as thick as soup. Even if the parish office had enough windows—which it hadn't—it wouldn't have made much difference.

Roberto had been given the Saturday morning shift in the church office, even though he'd explained to Father Pietro that it wasn't necessary to keep the office open on a Saturday. And sure enough, nobody had turned up. Those who hadn't gone to the beach didn't feel the need to brave the searing pavement and the glaring sun to come and ask for a baptism certificate or a wedding booking. Funerals, of course, were another matter, but it seemed that it was too hot even for the angel of death.

The only good thing was that, so long as nobody turned up, he could read his book on the philosophy of Saint Thomas Aquinas. Although Roberto felt a little bad about it, sometimes he didn't find parish life intellectually stimulating enough. He missed the philosophical and theological discussion he used to have in the seminary.

Still, the week at the summer camp had been fun. The only shadow on it was that the money had continued to go missing—even though they'd changed the storage place every night—so they had to give up on the trip to the botanic gardens and have a craft day in the parish hall instead.

The children had been as disappointed as him when he'd told them the trip was off. A feeling of anger was brewing in Roberto's heart, inflamed by the anxiety of finding the money to give the Cusumanos what they were owed.

More for an excuse to leave the stifling room than out of actual thirst, a hot and bothered Roberto decided to pop back home for a moment to get himself a glass of water to cool down his body and his mind.

The flat was unlocked. Strange. Father Pietro was usually out this time of day. Roberto slunk in like a cat, not sure who was he trying to catch.

"That's not enough money." He heard Mr Cavoli's voice.

He stopped just outside the dining room and peeped round the doorframe. Mr Cavoli and Father Pietro were sitting at the table, a spread of banknotes splayed out before them in piles.

Father Pietro sighed. "I'm sorry, this is all I've got."

He had been right about Mr Cavoli being a dodgy character! But what was Father Pietro doing with him? Had Mr Cavoli blackmailed him? Did Father Pietro have shady secrets?

"I can give you a lesser model."

"No, I want the best!"

"Then you'll have to find the money." Mr Cavoli scraped the chair on the floor and got up.

Roberto pulled back and crept out of the house with his heart shattered: Father Pietro, his role model, confidant and companion, wasn't what he'd thought. Back in the suffocating office, Roberto put his face in his hands and felt like crying.

The bishop would have to be informed, but what would he tell him? There were no hard facts, only snippets of conversations, impressions and suspicions.

Maybe he should confront Father Pietro. What if he was involved with the mafia?

As soon as the mafia knew that he was suspicious, they'd kill him.

There was a knock on the door. Roberto pulled himself up straight and answered, "Come in."

"Oh, hello, Mrs Grassi," he said with relief. "I thought you and your husband would be at the seaside for the weekend."

"Not these days. When we were younger and healthier, yes," she said, and a flicker of sadness crossed her face.

"What can I do for you?"

"Actually, I was looking for Father Pietro." Roberto's heart sank.

"He's not here," he said with sadness.

"Is everything all right?"

If anyone else had asked, Roberto would have just said, "I'm fine". But this was Mrs Grassi, and Roberto had a weight on his heart.

"Not really, no."

She came into the room, closed the door behind her and pulled out a chair.

"I'm feeling disappointed."

"Why?"

"Do you know what it's like when somebody you really trust turns out not to be as good and holy as you thought?"

"Yes."

"You've shared your work with this person, you've been a team together, and then, bam! That person betrays you. Maybe they've been doing things behind your back all along. Maybe, when you were sharing your thoughts and worries with them, they were already planning to hurt you. And you always thought that you could trust them like your own self."

A deep wrinkle formed on Mrs Grassi's forehead. "What do you mean?"

Roberto would have liked to get it all off his chest, but it wasn't professional to tell on a colleague, so to speak.

"I think I've found out who's stealing the summer camp money, and I won't say anything more."

All the suntan from the beach trip instantly drained off Mrs Grassi's face.

"Who?" she said, in a trembling voice.

"Somebody very close to me. Somebody

that I trusted very much. I'm sad beyond belief."

Mrs Grassi's lower lip trembled but not in the way it trembled when she was angry. She looked down at her hands, which were wringing the bottom of her shirt, and her eyelids glittered as if tears were bubbling over.

Her reaction seemed a bit over the top, and Roberto regretted his words.

She looked up into his eyes.

"I'm sorry," she managed to say.

Until then, Roberto had subconsciously hoped to be comforted by her, and now it looked like it was going to be the other way round!

He got up from his chair and put an arm around Mrs Grassi's shoulders.

"My husband is very sick. He needs an operation—in America—but we haven't got the money, so I started taking it. I was the one who got the grant from the mayor, so it was only fair, I thought."

"I beg your pardon?" Roberto asked.

Surely he had misheard.

"I'm sorry I upset you. That was the last thing I wanted to do. Cheating on the parish, Father Pietro, God—that's okay. If God sent this sickness to my husband despite all I do for this parish, He jolly well deserves that I take something back from Him. But I'm sorry to have lied to you."

This was not the comfort Roberto had hoped for when he opened his heart to Mrs Grassi. The mystery of the missing money was solved, but he didn't feel relieved.

Father Pietro hadn't stolen from the envelopes, but he still had dodgy dealings with Mr Cavoli, plus the woman he trusted like a mother had stolen, lied to him and was in the middle a faith crisis. Overall, it was a disaster.

The feeling of betrayal stung very much, but Roberto shook himself out of it and wiped his brow with a tissue.

"God didn't send any sickness to your husband. He's been smoking, drinking and eating badly all his life. He's brought it on himself. Why didn't you tell us about your husband? We would have organised some fundraising."

"He made me swear not to tell anyone. He fears that he might have his taxi licence revoked if the news of his heart problem gets to the licencing people. Plus, he knows that Mr Cavoli is buzzing around me, and he doesn't want him to consider me a widow before time."

"Mr Cavoli is going on a marital counselling weekend with his wife. I don't think he will harass you anymore. Anyway, so long as you love your husband and not Mr Cavoli, your husband has nothing to fear. Other than you ending up in prison for doing something silly for him!"

Then Mrs Grassi burst into tears again.

"Please, forgive me, Roberto," she pleaded, grabbing his hand.

"I forgive you, Angela. And I think I'm allowed to say that God forgives you too."

***

It hadn't occurred to Roberto that buses would be as scarce as locals in the August heat. He waited over an hour before one finally showed up. This was an extra aggravation that he really didn't need: visiting the Cusumanos after all that had happened was hard enough.

Plan A consisted of apologising to them and handing them the cash Mrs Grassi had returned. Plan B—in the event they wouldn't receive him because they were still cross with him—was to slip the cash, inside an envelope, through their letterbox with a note.

The journey, however, took less time than Roberto expected, as the roads were deserted. He wondered if he would actually find the Cusumanos at the theatre, but then he guessed that they probably didn't have the money to go away on a holiday.

Much to his surprise, tourists were crowding outside the theatre and more were arriving every minute, armed with smartphones and city guides.

Then Roberto remembered that he had written an English review of the puppet show he had attended and had posted it online.

Mrs Cusumano scuttled out of the ticketing booth towards Roberto and spoke with tears in her eyes.

"Thank you so much for whatever you wrote! A lot of tourists have come to us saying that they'd read about us on the internet. Please, Father, take back your book and come in, the show's about to start!"

***

There was a long queue outside the parish office so Roberto was surprised when the door opened without him having yet called in the next person.

But it was Father Pietro.

"The bishop called to say that he wants to see you in his office this afternoon at three," he said, and popped back out as quickly as he had popped in, leaving a trail of questions.

Why did the bishop want to see him? Had Father Pietro told the bishop lies about him to get him out of the picture and carry on with whatever he was involved in, without witnesses? It was definitely time to tell the bishop about Father Pietro's secretive dealings, however much he hated doing so.

***

"Your Excellency, good afternoon," Roberto said, entering the bishop's office.

He bowed low to apologise for his lateness. Although he'd left home with plenty of time to spare, the first bus had been too full and he'd had to wait for another one.

He already felt extremely anxious about what he had to tell the bishop about Father Pietro, and now his lateness made him even more uncomfortable.

The imposing look of the bishop's office didn't help: a large room with a tall frescoed ceiling. Oil paintings of unsmiling bishops looked down from the walls onto ancient leather chairs with carved bowed legs.

It looked pompous and rich but slightly dilapidated. Old wealth, new poverty, Roberto reflected, thinking about his parish's roof-repair issues.

"Just call me Father, please. I hate formalities. Come and take a seat," the bishop said cordially, offering him a chair. "I'm sorry for calling you so abruptly. I won't take much of your time and will go straight to the point. I've heard about your successes as summer

camp leader. The trips, the theatre workshop…
I gather that you like working with young
people, am I correct?"

He didn't at the beginning, but he did now.
"Very much!" he replied.

"Good. Those were primary school kids, if
I'm not mistaken. How do you like working
with teens?"

"I like that too."

"And how do you find the parish of the
Ascension?"

Why was the bishop asking these questions?
Was he thinking of transferring him? Had
Father Pietro anticipated him by lodging a
complaint before he spilled the beans on him?

A few months earlier, Roberto would have
jumped at the chance to move to another
parish, one with fewer problems and more
intellectual stimulation. But a pang of sadness
now struck him at the thought of leaving the
parish of the Ascension. If anyone should be
the one to go, it should be Father Pietro-with
his dodgy money dealings-not him!

"I very much enjoy working there."

"Good. Because Father Pietro and your
parishioners, I hear, would not like to see you
go. But this might present a problem."

What? Father Pietro didn't want him to go?
Roberto was confused.

"You see," the bishop continued, searching Roberto's eyes, "about a year ago, the Jesuits in Rettona asked me if I could spare somebody to teach philosophy at their school. They'd looked within their ranks but couldn't find anyone who was comfortable teaching philosophy to children as young as eight all the way to teens. You've been our seminary's top philosophy student so I immediately thought of you, but I wasn't sure that you had enough experience of children. So I assigned you to the parish of the Ascension and asked Father Pietro to give you as much exposure to the young ones as he could. I made it very clear to Father Pietro that you were not his 'to keep', so to speak. Now, after Father Pietro's glowing report on how you've managed the summer camp, I think you're ready to teach at the Jesuits' school. But if you don't wish to leave the parish of the Ascension, we have a logistics problem, because the school is on the opposite side of town. Assuming, of course, that you would like to take up this teaching post. Wouldn't you?"

What game was Father Pietro playing? Still, Roberto couldn't believe his ears: he'd be working with young people, reading, studying, learning and teaching the subject he loved!

"I'd be delighted to take up the post!" he

said.

Not only did he enjoy working with young people, but he loved philosophy. Plus, he already had in mind two urgent causes to which he'd be more than happy to donate his teacher's salary.

"Good. But can you get from your parish to the school every morning?"

Roberto swallowed hard. Now was the time to ask for it. Could he do it?

"It would be no problem if I had a scooter…"

The bishop's eyebrows jolted.

"I hope you didn't mind me suggesting it. I've seen a second-hand scooter in the paper for only one hundred euros…" Roberto stammered.

The bishop kept silently raising his eyebrows up towards what had once been his hairline. Then he burst into a chuckle.

"How could I not have thought of it! I'd been struggling to work out a solution and it was right under my nose. You see, only a little while ago, Father Pietro asked me for some money to buy you a scooter. He'd already collected quite a lot from your parishioners— especially a man who sells cars and scooters, I understand."

Roberto felt dizzy. Father Pietro and Mr

Cavoli's mysterious money dealings were nothing other than a collection to buy him a scooter! Roberto felt tears bubbling in his eyes—tears of relief, gratitude and shame at the same time.

"I had told him to wait till the end of the summer," the bishop continued, "and now it is the end of the summer. So a scooter you'll have. But, Roberto?"

"Yes, Your Excellency," Roberto said, his voice shaking with emotion.

"You would be sorely missed if you were to… I mean, you'll ride carefully, won't you?"

The End

All books by Stefania Hartley

In this series:

Father Roberto and the Missing Money
Father Roberto and the Runaway Ring
Father Roberto and the Rural Riots
Father Roberto and the Mystery of the Microscope

Short Stories Collections:

Tales from the Parish

Father Okoli dreams of owning a flock of hens and studying for a PhD, when his bishop saddles him with yet another parish to look after. But as Father moves to Moreton-on-the-Edge, a farming village in the English Cotswolds, he's plugged into a community of warm-hearted characters, from the motherly parish secretary to her septuagenarian neighbour who's become a cycling champion, and from teenagers requiring driving lessons to atheist publicans who believe in miracles.

As the community pulls together to reopen the village's Electric Picture House, dreams are fulfilled, teen love blossoms and Father

Okoli feels that Moreton-on-the-Edge is now home.

Good Habits

Sister Luce loves her quiet life in the convent in the Italian Apennine mountains. In the company of her hens, among chestnut groves and fir forests, the shy young nun is at her happiest. But Mother Speranza has invited a TV crew into their convent to shoot a documentary about their life, and she asks Sister Luce to be the convent's poster girl.

Never has Sister Luce's vow of obedience been so sorely tested, especially when four worldly women come to share the convent's life under the camera's lens.

Between a Santa dash and a carnival float, a forest sit-in and a song competition, Sister Luce becomes performer, protester, agony aunt and equestrian nun as she learns to conquer her fears.

The Season to Be Jolly

Will Melina be able to give up her role as Christmas cook this year? Riccardo always looks out for the same person at Christmas Mass, but what will he do now that she's actually appeared? Mummy and Daddy keep getting presents through the post but they don't know who's sending them. How can they find out? Ten humorous and heartwarming short stories brimming with Sicilian sunshine and mountain snow, fragrant with freshly baked panettone and ringing with Christmas bells, perfect for the festive season.

Sweet Surprises

Does Raffaella's prospective husband only send half-length photos because he has something to hide? How can Don Pericle help a bride who's too shy to walk down the aisle? While Giovanna entrusts her search for a love match to pheromones and Melina despairs about Tanino being stuck at home with her, a donkey saves the day for a farmer's neighbours and the class's naughty boy turns over a new leaf thanks to a misunderstanding.

Keeping it Cool

Every good mum knows how to keep her daughter safe. But how will Izzy's mum cope on a visit to a perilous ice rink? Josh thinks Elise's boyfriend wish list is rather unusual. Can he tick all the boxes? Mario knows that his name is as common in Italy as John Smith. But why are his friends sending him funeral wreaths?

Sand, Sea & Tamburello

When Rosetta dries her hair on her balcony, she's not interested in the sun's warmth but in the young fishmonger who's eager to warm her heart. Can Don Pericle be a gracious host when an entire wedding party gets stranded at his villa?

A Season of Goodwill

How far should Viviana's family go to avoid being thirteen at the table? Should Melina and Tanino attend a New Year's party hosted by Melina's old flame? Why do Don Pericle's clients want a Christmas wedding at all costs?

To Be Loved

Amanda's name means "to be loved" and she's taken it as her duty to make herself lovable, but it's hard work. Has Tanino really abandoned Melina at home to freeze? Mark hasn't seen Nora for thirty years and, since then, he's lost a leg and all his hair. If he wasn't enough for her then, can he be now? What happens if the dating app's algorithms go haywire?

Drive Me Crazy

"Cohabitation is tribulation" goes an Italian

saying, and after more than fifty years of married life, Tanino and Melina know a thing or two about the challenges of living together. Follow their antics as they compete to give their grandchild the best birthday present, struggle to lose some extra weight, and try to make it to their godchild's christening on time in this collection of twelve short stories dedicated entirely to the much-loved Sicilian couple from the pages of The People's Friend magazine.

Stars Are Silver
Is it too late for Melina to learn to drive? Is Don Pericle's vow never to fall in love again still valid after fifty years? Will a falling piano squash Filomena or just shake up her heart? Why does the mother of the bride ask Don Pericle to cancel the wedding?

A Slip of the Tongue
Will Melina regret faking to be sick to avoid her chores? Can Don Pericle organise a wedding for a groom who doesn't know? Who has stolen the marble pisces from the cathedral's floor?

Fresh from the Sea
Will Gnà Peppina give her customers what

they need, even if it's more than food? What pleasures can a man indulge in after his wife has put him on a draconian diet? Who will be able to cook dinner for the family with five euros?

Confetti and Lemon Blossom
For Don Pericle, wedding organising is a calling, not just a career. Deep in the Sicilian countryside, between rose gardens and trellised balconies, up marble staircases and across damasked ballrooms, these charming stories unfold: stories of star-crossed love, of comedic misunderstandings and of deep friendships, of love triumphing in the face of adversity.

What's Yours is Mine
Can Melina give away her husband's possessions because they've always said that 'what's mine is yours and what's yours is mine'? Will the 'Sleep Doctor' deliver on his promises? How will the young Sicilian duke, Pericle, help his friend get married?

Short Romances:

How to Choose a Husband

Grazia Colonna has waited fifty years to meet The One. Now that her best friend is getting married for the second time, Grazia is sure that she'll meet The One at Rebecca's wedding. He will sweep Grazia off her feet and snatch her from the clutches of her bullying mother. But first Grazia needs to alter the dress she will wear at the event and, for this, she needs the help of the village's grumpy widower tailor, Hector Gonzales.

As the bride is stuck abroad and may not get back in time for the wedding, Grazia and Hector are forced to work together and, inconveniently, they fall in love.

Can they ensure that the right wedding goes ahead and the wrong one doesn't?

The Italian Fake Date

When Alice Baker discovers that she's been adopted, she knows she won't have peace until she's found her Italian birth mother. But all she has is a letter written twenty-five years ago and an old address.

Jaded about love and unable to forgive his ex-fiancée and his brother, Paolo Rondino is struggling to find inspiration for a sculpture that will make or break his career. Hoping that a trip home will help him find his muse again, he decides to return to Italy, even if this means confronting the two people who betrayed him.

Alice and Paolo strike a deal: he will help her find her birth mother and she will pretend to be his girlfriend to please his mother. It looks like the perfect exchange, until real feelings start to grow…

Sweet Competition for Camillo's Café

Camillo runs a popular café on Altavicia's main square. Giada runs an equally popular café across the square. They have both entered Altavicia's Best Café competition.

Scarred by his father's death, Camillo's greatest wish is to escape the Calabrian seaside village and return to his beloved London, where his family was last together and happy. Abandoned by her parents, Giada's greatest wish is to earn her nonna's love. The competition trophy is the ticket to both their dreams, but only one can win.

As Camillo discovers that happiness doesn't come from a location and Giada that love isn't earned, can enemies become friends, and maybe more?

Second Chances at Mamma's Trattoria

When Eleonora got a job at Mamma Cristina's trattoria, she didn't tell the sweet old woman that she was her son's ex-wife, nor that the twins are her granddaughters. Her plan was to give the twins a taste of family life without any of the trouble. But she had not planned for Davide to come home.

Davide loves his job at sea and he wouldn't have come home if it hadn't been for Mamma Cristina's health scare. The last thing he expected to find was his ex-wife implanted in the heart of his home with two young daughters in tow.

The last thing Eleonora and Davide want is to work together. But a celebrity Christmas wedding at the trattoria requires every hand on deck. How long can Eleonora and Davide avoid each other while working together and living under the same roof?

Under Far Eastern Skies

Everyone thinks that thirty-one-year-old Shona Wells should get married: her overbearing father, her starry-eyed little sister, and the whole expat community in 1930s Singapore. But Shona wants independence and the freedom to choose her own way, to travel the world exploring nature.

The last thing twenty-five-year old Will Palmer needs is marriage. He's too busy discovering new plant species in the remotest jungles in the world.

But then, three days before Shona is due to sail back to England, she meets Will, and finds someone with the same passion for the natural world. They are perfect for each other, until a series of misadventures and misunderstandings threatens to pull them apart forever.

Welcome to Quayside

Forty-year-old Tanya Baker dreams of starting a new life and making friends when she moves to a block of flats by the River Thames with her thirteen-year-old daughter, Hattie. But as Tanya and Hattie knock on neighbours' doors in search of a tin opener, it's clear that the residents of Number One Quayside like to keep to themselves.

Everyone, that is, except their next-door neighbours, Italian chef Giacomo Dalamo, and his thirteen-year-old daughter, Frankie.

Between a delicious dish of lasagne (Giacomo's) and a burnt salad (Tanya's), they hatch a plan to set up a library of things in their building, so that residents can borrow rarely-used items, from DIY tools to sports equipment and party supplies. As all the residents at Quayside pull together to make the library happen, dreams are fulfilled, a community is born and love blossoms again.

ABOUT THE AUTHOR

Stefania was born in Sicily and immediately started growing, but not very much. She left her sunny island after falling head over heels in love with an Englishman, and now she lives in the UK with her husband and their three children.

Having finally learnt English, she's enjoying it so much that she now writes novels and short stories which have been longlisted, shortlisted, commended, and won prizes.

If you have enjoyed these stories, please leave a review. To be the first to hear when she's releasing a new book, sign up for her newsletter and receive an exclusive short story: www.stefaniahartley.com/subscribe

www.ingramcontent.com/pod-product-compliance
Lightning Source LLC
Chambersburg PA
CBHW072034170626
46811CB00008B/3068